WE HAVE LIFT-OFF!

WE HAVE LIFT-OFF!

by **Sean Taylor**

Illustrated by
Hannah Shaw

F
FRANCES LINCOLN
CHILDREN'S BOOKS

You're looking at the first chicken in outer space,
which was me. You see, I used to live on
Mr Tanner's Farm. And it really was a right old dump.

Mr Tanner poisoned
the air with smoke,

and filled the river with junk,

and cut down all the trees,

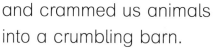

and crammed us animals
into a crumbling barn.

But his house just kept getting
bigger and **bigger** and **bigger!**

We animals couldn't take it any more.

So we held a meeting in a top-secret location,
to see if there was anything we could do.

And we decided to do something!

We built an intergalactic rocket so that we could escape, away from Mr Tanner, and up to the clear, clean stars. It was a difficult plan.
But if it worked, we were sure that news would spread.

Then animals all round the world
would start doing the same thing!
Because, let's face it, animals have had enough
of trying to share our planet with people.
People just keep on messing things up.

The pig who designed
our rocket reckoned it
was strong enough
to carry us all.
But he said someone
had go on a
test flight.

And that was when I got chosen!

I was given moon boots,
a space helmet and a map.
And a supply of cornflakes
that looked enough to
last for a whole life.

START   EMERGENCY
         ABANDON
         MISSION

I was shown the start button
(which I was supposed to press at the start).
And the emergency abandon mission button
(which I wasn't supposed to press, except in
an emergency).

Then, 5 - 4 - 3 - 2 - 1 . . .
we have lift off!

Up I went . . . away from the litter and clutter of
Mr Tanner's farm!

First of all, everything went fine.
I was in radio contact with the Flight
Director at animal mission control.

And I was on
my way to the
stars!

But there was
a problem.

I was holding the map upside-down. And suddenly
the rocket was heading back towards our planet.

"Don't come back!" said the Flight Director.
But it was too late. The rocket was the wrong way
round, and the only way was down.

We had to do another test flight and this time a very clever rabbit was chosen.

He put on moon boots and a space helmet, and he was given a map and a big box of carrots.

Then, 5 - 4 - 3 - 2 - 1 . . .
we have lift off!

Up went the rabbit . . . out of the smog and smoke
of Mr Tanner's farm!

First of all everything went fine.
The rabbit was on his way to the stars!
Then there was a problem. I think the rabbit got
nervous. He started eating carrots very fast . . .

. . . and the box got stuck over his head.
He bumped the steering wheel and the rocket started
heading back. "Don't come back!" said the Flight
Director. But it was too late. The rabbit couldn't get
the box off, and the only way was down.

We still had to
do a successful
test flight,
and a very calm
sheep was
chosen next.

She was given moon boots, a space helmet, a map
and a supply of cabbage leaves in little boxes that
she couldn't get stuck over her head.

Then, 5 - 4 - 3 - 2 - 1 . . .
we have lift off!

Up went the sheep . . . away from the muck and junk
of Mr Tanner's farm!

First of all, everything
went fine.
The sheep was
on her way to
the stars!

Then there was a problem.
The sheep fell asleep.

What's worse, she leant her head on the emergency
abandon mission button so the rocket turned
automatically back.
"For Goodness' sake!" said the Flight Director.
"Don't come back!"

But it was too late. The sheep was asleep, and the
only way was down.

And that was when Mr Tanner came to find out
what the noise was about . . . and he discovered
our rocket! He seemed to think it was funny because
he laughed at it.

Then he just looked inside, as if it was his.
But the joke was on him, because somehow he
pressed the start button.

Then, 5 - 4 - 3 - 2 - 1 . . .
we have lift off!

Up went Mr Tanner . . . on his way to the stars.

And we never saw him again!

It wasn't what we'd planned. But actually it was better than trying to escape in the rocket.

And news has spread. Now animals all round the world are building intergalactic rockets and sending

people like Mr Tanner up to the stars.
So if you're one of the people who makes a mess of our planet, watch out!
It could be your turn next!

More great TIME TO READ books to collect:

978-1-84780-476-1

978-1-84780-475-4

978-1-84780-477-8

978-1-84780-478-5

Frances Lincoln titles are available from all good bookshops.
You can also buy books and find out more about your favourite titles,
authors and illustrators on our website: www.franceslincoln.com